The Life of a Book

The Life of a Book

• • •

Danial Suits

Copyright © 2010 Danial Suits
All rights reserved, including the rights to reproduce this book or portions thereof in any form whatsoever. For more information address Suits Publishing at 22660 I-30 Lot 33 Bryant, Arkansas 72022
This paperback edition October 2010
10 9 8 7 6 5 4 3 2 1

ISBN-13: 9780615425559
ISBN-10: 0615425550

Table of Contents

Jason Simpson

● ● ●

THE LIFE OF A BOOK began with an author. The thoughts from the book started with the finishing of the last pages. The author put the book through publishing, did the book signing and a copy of the book went to a library where anyone could check it out and read it. And so the journey began…

Day one. This was the first day at a public library. People were all around checking out different books. A few people passed me by. The author gave me a catchy title, a fun title. This library had books old and new for people of different ages to enjoy.

A young mom and her son were in the children's section. This is where I was; in the children's section where it is fun for kids. The mom picked me up while talking with her son. She smiled as she opened up my cover to show her son my pictures. The son was four years old. The mom checked my card out with the librarian. The family was good for two weeks. We took a long ride to their house.

On the way to their house, I was riding with family-friendly videos for their viewing pleasure. When they got home, the mother picked up the bag that I was in. The videos went downstairs on the shelf with the other videos. I wound up in the kids room with the other kids' books.

The difference was that I was new compared to them. The kid's name was Jason Simpson. He was learning to read and his mom helped him by reading him bedtime stories. It was the main thing that I was good for. I sat on the shelf for a night.

The next night, she took me off the shelf. It was time for his reading lesson. They opened my cover as soon as she tucked him in. While I was on the same shelf as some of the other books, I was not being held up by a book end. I was easily spotted. I was the favorite for a couple of weeks.

Jason really enjoyed his mother reading me to him. She smiled as she was reading from her chair and watched him doze off. At that point I found that some kids may not finish me in one night. I hoped that in the coming days, he would be able to know how I ended.

In Jason's neighborhood, it was sometimes cloudy. His dad was home for the weekend but they could not play ball. The forecast was calling for rain. Jason's dad was a salesman and sometimes took road trips that made him leave town.

Jason wanted to spend some time with his dad. When his dad asked him what he wanted to do, Jason pointed to me indicating he wanted to continue reading lessons. His dad looked at his watch and found it was about time for Jason's nap. His mom was at the store so dad went to lie on the couch and asked Jason to bring his book over.

Jason pulled me off the shelf for a second time and his dad began to read me. His dad asked him where he and his mom left off. The only thing that Jason could remember was the last thing he heard. They opened me up and Jason led his dad to the spot he thought they should start from.

They read one more section of me and Jason headed off to sleep one more time. This kid may not get done with me anytime soon.

His dad put him to bed. When the mom got home, he updated her about me and she nodded in agreement. He put me back on the shelf for another day.

Over the next few days, Jason had one last chance to finish me before I had to go back. Jason and his mom got together. They got me off the shelf and sat on the couch. Jason cuddled up to her ready for the story to start.

Jason finally heard "The End". I knew that my job here was done and I had to go back tomorrow.

Jason's mom began the preparations for the trip. I was part of a list of errands. Jason had to go to school so he was not going to the library with his mom this time. He was the first drop off.

I was returned to the library and got checked back in.

Back At Home

ONE OF THE NICE THINGS about the library was the nice ride back to the shelf. I got to ride the book cart without paying admission. That's good news to me all the way around.

I was not alone in this feeling. Most of these other books were the same way. About 13 to 25 other books were accompanying me on this cart.

You should have heard the compliments some of these books were giving. They were quite nice. We got to turn different directions.

The rush of the wind from whichever direction the person was pushing, plus the view of the ceiling where we were was splendid. The ceiling kept going and going and wait…we were going backwards. It was time for a different rush of wind.

There we went again. We were playing musical spots. For every spot and turn of direction we made, the cart lost one of us. Just think of how the cart pusher felt.

The person who pushed us around to our shelves sometimes enjoyed what they were doing. Sometimes the person was a girl and sometimes it was a boy.

There were about three of these pushers from what I could see from the shelf.

Katlin Wagner

● ● ●

IT SEEMED TO BE TIME for my next family involvement. This time a father and daughter had picked me up from the shelves. More sets of fingerprints came onto my covers. That day, there was a different librarian. Opening the back of my cover, she slipped out my index card, and stamped it with a two week expiration date.

Katlin Wagner was a ballerina. She loved to play with batons in her tutu. I sat on the shelf. This shelf was different from the other two that I was on. The girl had me lying on the shelf on my backside. She was six years old.

This was a new position for me. The shelf was not new; I could tell. Either that or someone had put it in upside down. I am glad that I am a hard cover. The shelf feels a little on the rough side. Until the time comes for them to move me for reading, I have to stay like this.

This day was coming to an end. Katlin had to put her things away so that her parents would be able to walk without running into anything. Katlin was a little sad at that point because she had to stop what she was doing. Ballet was her life for all of her six years. Going to bed was the last thing on her mind.

The sun was down and she got into bed. Her dad came in and pulled me off the shelf. Her dad picked up a chair in one hand and me in the other. Right then I felt a little squeezed; as if words would fall off my pages. He opened me up and began to put her to sleep.

Katlin woke up the next morning and got ready for school. She grabbed me from the shelf and wanted her parents to let her take me to school. Mom and Dad shook their heads in disagreement and wanted her to hand the book over.

She tried to insist a couple of times. Dad came back with a stern "No." At six years old, who knows what could happen to me if they let her take me. She finally gave me to her parents in defeat.

I felt a little safer now. Her parents headed back upstairs to the daughter's room and set me back onto the shelf. This is where I stayed for a few hours until she would return home.

Time passed by and Katlin finally got back home. She saw her mom in the kitchen while dad was in the study. I saw her coming into the room. Dropping offer her bag, she spent some time in the bathroom. I saw a lot from this shelf such as the cars going back and forth out the window.

I saw the most at night when Katlin went to bed and when dad picked me off the shelf. He was able to get through another section of me with her. She dozed off to sleep. The dad turned off the reading light and left the night light on. This was when I got the most of my sleep and rest: when they put me back onto the shelf. This time, I was leaning up against the shelf wall.

During the next few days, Katlin pulled me off the shelf from her room and we headed downstairs. She laid me on the counter top face up in order to read me in front of her mom who was cooking. She sometimes had a hard time saying some of the words while reading them aloud. Her mom would come over to help her.

Dad came in sometimes to listen to his daughter read me aloud. He was usually on an errand when he was out of his office. He grinned at his daughter's progress as he acknowledged the three of us here. The daughter learned to read with my help. A few hours later, it was night time again. Mom came to tuck her in. She walked over to me and brought me to where she was going to sit.

Katlin's mom read me to her daughter as she dozed off to sleep. The mom soon found it was time to resume my position back on the shelf. This shelf routine was getting to be a pretty normal thing. The time was coming again for me to be going. I hoped that she would get a chance to finish me before that happened.

In the next couple of days, Katlin finished reading me with her parents. This was my second family in a few months. So far, I was helping kids learn how to read while visiting their homes. It seemed a little cloudy that tonight. I hoped it was not this way in the morning.

It was morning on the day I needed to go back. A look at the clouds told me that I may get damaged from the weather. It looked like it might rain that day. I had hoped that she found protection for me so that I wouldn't get damaged.

Here she came with her purse. It was big enough for me to get in. I had hoped that was what she was putting me in. I was right. Man, it was dark in there. After a couple of speed bumps, we got back to the library.

Jerry Peterson

• • •

A FEW MONTHS HAD PASSED and I then got some attention from a father and his son. The father picked me up from the shelf and handed me to his son. From the feel of it, the son was about eight years old. His grip was softer compared to his dad. And smaller.

Jerry was a nice little boy who loved his dad very much. While the two of them went out and played catch, I sat on the shelf in another room. At least this shelf was more comfortable than the last one that I was on. I had my tour of the third house and met the covers of a neighboring book.

The sky was a little different from here. The air conditioning worked so I didn't have to worry about disappearing ink. His father wanted only the best for his son and to make things fun for him at the same time.

When Jerry was bored, he would take me off the shelf and start to read me. His reading was at a medium level. It was fine for his age but, at the same time, he could have used some improvement. He read me aloud while his dad listened to him. I think his dad was in the next room.

It was snowing outside. I sure hoped my hard cover would give me some comfort for the next few months. Wait a minute. The heat in the house was adjusting the temperature in here. That was a close call.

It was dark outside. Jerry was heading to bed. His father came in and tucked him in. The father figured that he already had enough reading for one day. I saw him say good night to his son. This was another day gone by.

Tomorrow, the boy could finish reading me. At least, he hoped he could. But as the next day came, trouble arose in the house and he never got to finish me. Those two weeks flew by and I never got the chance to let him read the rest of me. His father was coming to take me away back to the library.

At least his house was temperature controlled to the point that I didn't lose any ink.

Joseph Anderson

JOSEPH ANDERSON'S TWO PARENTS LOOKED like they worked a lot. They had grabbed me off the shelf for their son to read, which was fine by me. This was another house for me to visit. Joseph was only three years old and was still wondering what life was all about.

If they began reading me, I could help Joseph by giving him a good starting point for his imagination. The regular librarian was on shift. She knew what she was doing. She stamped my card and massaged my back cover by putting the card back in. That always felt good to me.

Their car had a lot of stuff in it that I thought should be in a storage place. I could tell that this family was not very organized. They had things scattered from one end of the car to the other.

I was feeling a little nervous about this. I sure hoped the house was in better condition than this car. It was a few minutes for the ride home until we finally got to the driveway. I thought it was the driveway. It turned out that it was a corner curb; we had turned and that made me think it was a driveway. The car turned onto a side street and parked on the road. I looked around the area and from my view, I could see a lot of work going on.

The house looked like it was in pieces from the outside. Going to the inside, almost everything needed repair. It wasn't as if these people were poor or anything like that but just that they were remodeling. One might have to guess the actual reason that they checked me out. A moment later, I saw it. There stood a three-year-old boy who needed some reading education. When the boy took me to his room, there was a stack of books that I landed on with his help.

It was obvious that the stack was not going to be there too long. A few minutes later, I found that I was right. The parents had picked up my stack.

There was another book lying on top of me so they did not know I was there. It seemed the stack was in the way a little bit. The stack I was with went into some kind of closet. I seemed to have been forgotten about because some time has passed since I had been placed in here.

By now, someone should have found me. I was sure that they had lost me. I was getting worried about my expiration date now. I saw the lights going on and off periodically. This went on a lot as time flew by. It felt like six months have flown by.

Suddenly, hey look, someone was opening the door. I felt a lifting motion. That meant that I was moving. Wow. I think I just landed on a table. The book on top of had been picked up. I was able to see the rest of my surroundings now.

Looking around, I saw a different environment. The house was fixed up. There were finished floors downstairs that I could see from my upstairs view. The mom looked at me and opened my back cover. She seemed to have called someone over to me to look at me.

It seemed as though they realized that I was past my expiration date. They were worried about what kind of bill they would have to pay. Surely they got a bill from my library about my cost.

Here came the husband with a return trip to the table and he was holding a document with an envelope. It looked from my place like a past due notice. The mom was getting her check book ready for my return.

I could see her getting ready to run an errand. Wow, it looked like he was going with her. They may have to explain my disappearance. This might be quite a trip.

I could normally feel the road way back to the library, but something was different. This didn't seem like the same return trip to the library. They were probably going to do something else before dropping me off.

Boy was I wrong. As they brought me to a library, it wasn't the one I normally went to. This trip was different. It seemed that the library had moved since I was gone. Just when I was getting used to those other books beside me the library moved. It looked much bigger now.

We were on the inside. The parents were talking with the librarian about me. The mom looked like she was making out a check for my bill. She handed it to the librarian. My short worries seemed to be over.

The librarian replaced the card in the back of my cover with an updated one. That always felt good to me. I was placed in a new place to make new friends.

Smith Davis

ANOTHER KIDS' PARENTS CAME BY about three weeks later. They took me off the shelf and checked me out. Yippee, another kid to help out! Another home to visit. Another family to get to know. This kid was about 5 years old. We got into the car with their other things. This was a nice comfortable ride. They had a nice place to live and it was a two story home. I wondered if it had anything to do with how many books they might have on their shelves.

When they got home, I wound up in the kids room. Although it was nice sitting on a finished shelf, I noticed one thing in common with where I always landed. That was in the kid's room. I have never been in the parent's room. There must have been something to that. Here, again, I landed in the kid's room.

Sometime in the evening, the family got together. They pulled me from the shelf in the kid's room and instead of taking me to the kid's bed for a bed time story, we went down stairs to the family room. The four of us cuddled up in a bundle in the corner of the couch; everyone's hands on me. What a massage!

They were giggling and laughing and joking and having fun with the way I was reading. That made that trip quite an event. Both the parents were in on it. To them, there was nothing better than spending time with their five-year-old son.

The next day, Smith's friends were on their way over. Not only did he have loving parents who liked to spend time with him, but he also had a lot of friends. There were lots of electronic gadgets in his room here. They must be coming to play with them.

Little did I know that instead of playing with all the electronic gadgets, they took me off the shelf to read. Smith started sharing me around and letting the other boys take a look at me. He must be one popular kid in this area. I wondered if he was just a little too young for school. The boys started to read me to each other. I didn't know I was in such demand to be read. I really made these boys proud of themselves.

It is a little later in the day. The boys had to go home and prepare for their evening meals. Smith put me back on the shelf. Well, he was almost done with me. I guess he wanted to finish me with his parents. He went to follow his friends and prepare to eat his dinner. This was a really nice house.

Soon it would be time for me to leave again. But one thing that I thought would be for certain was that the kid was most likely going to finish me. It looked promising. It became bed time. Smith had to get ready for bed. His mom came into the room to get him tucked in. She came over to my book case to get me off the shelf and we went over to the bed.

She started reading me to him. He listened to her as much as he could before he started to fall asleep. He wanted to hear the end of my story. Luckily, since she just got to the end of me, he was able to hear "The End" from his mom. This meant that I was done here.

It was the next morning. It was time for me to go back to the library. Mom started to pack up some things to go. She and her husband made a trip to the library while their son was in pre-school. The librarian who checked me out with these parents must have been on lunch. I have not seen this other one before. He might be a new trainee. A lot can happen in a couple of weeks.

Jefferson Jackson

• • •

ABOUT A MONTH HAD PASSED since anyone took a notice of me. I sat on this shelf for a while and thought that maybe I was losing my appeal. Sometimes, when a book sat on the shelf for a while, it would begin to get unhappy. It is then, at that time, someone would come by and pick me off the shelf. You just never know when someone will be interested in you.

There was one exception. This time, the kid in this family was not really interested in me. This kid didn't seem interested much in reading in general. The parents took me off the shelf anyway. We went up to the counter so that I could get checked out. The kid kept staring someplace else. I was able to notice what the kid was staring at. There was a child's play place at the other end of the library.

I wasn't getting the needed attention from the kid. The parents took care of that problem by making him do what he was told. The kid had a nice attitude after that. When we got to their house, the kid went to his room. I soon followed but not in his hands. Rather, I was in the hands of the parents. The kid was not a very good reader and toys were more important to him, so the parents got some of their exercise by settling him down. By the time he'd been settled down, they were sometimes too tired to read me to him. I took the shelf for my night's sleep.

This family spent more time trying to settle down the kid than getting anything done in the house. The next morning, the parents got up to take care of the morning rituals. Mom got her child up and ready for breakfast. Dad was getting ready for work. After a couple of hours, it was time for the kid to go to school. The child always had play on his mind. It would surprise me if the kid does not get into trouble at school.

At the end of the day, dad got home first and prepared himself a snack. He seemed to know what was coming. His son often did his homework in his room. This must be why dad was placing his snacks in the room on the desk. The mom was heading out to pick him up from school.

Dad was setting up the stuff in the room when his son came in for his studies. Mom was in the kitchen fixing dinner. Dad tried everything he could to settle the kid down. He never would leave the kid's side because he knew the homework would not get done. It took him a few hours to get through the first few lessons. By this time, it seemed to be dinner time because they left the area.

About an hour later, the dad continued to go over the homework with the son. He hoped that the son would outgrow this stage of wildness. It was very evident that the boy was not going to have time for me. If anybody was going to read me, it would be mom.

It was too late into the evening for reading to be done. Dad had decided that it was time for bed and they called it a day. I remained on the shelf for the night.

One of the main problems was that I had to go back sometime soon or I'd be overdue. A person would not want to be late about returning me. It was the next morning; the usual ritual was here for the boy. It was time for him to go back to school. Mom came in after dropping the kid off to school while dad was at work. She picked me off the shelf and started reading my pages.

A couple of hours later, she finished reading me and started to gather a few things together. I am glad that she enjoyed my pages but, normally, I was there for the kids.

One thing was certain, no matter what house I was in, an adventure was always present. Mom put a few things into the car and I was one of them. She was evidently trying to run a few errands. She returned me to the library and I was picked up by the librarian and checked back in.

Sam Colton

• • •

SAM WAS A GO-GETTER. WHEN this kid wanted something, he tried everything he could to get it. Even though he wanted to achieve all his goals, he kept his morals and ethics straight as they were taught to him. I learned this after he picked me off the shelf a few weeks after the last drop off. It wasn't the parents who picked me off the shelf, it was the kid himself. He didn't do it with a hint of misery but rather with self-excitement.

His parents were the ones who wanted to wait for a little bit. The kid insisted and won. They had gone through the checkout and made their way to their car. The family gathered their merchandise into the car and drove off. I had some fun traveling in some of these cars. Some of the rides were more comfortable than others were. Nevertheless, they felt nice and the air conditioning was a nice touch.

On the way home, Sam wanted to start reading me right away. Though he had difficulty doing this because the bags, where I was, were behind his seat; his parents knew what he was thinking. Occasionally, dad looked back in the rear view mirror and noticed his son's facial expressions. The dad seemed eager to get home so his son could start reading.

While mom was putting away the groceries, she had her husband in the living room with the son and I. They were reading me so that the son would be happy. It seemed that fulfilling a dream or desire for a kid was a special gift. Some people may believe that doing this may spoil the kid but doing this really kept the kid active with the parents. One of the things Sam enjoyed doing was accomplishing things as soon as he could. It seemed to come natural to him.

His parents believed that their son would go far in life because of how hard he tried for things. It only took them a day and a half to read through me. That was amazing because that just didn't happen. People normally would take at least a week and a half to read me. In that case, I started to think I would miss this kid because of how smart he was. Each of his parents complimenting their own side of the family for the intelligence level. Sometimes that was funny in itself.

However, to my surprise, the parents kept me on the shelf for a few more days. My guess was that not only was I daily reading material, but bed time reading material as well. They wanted to read me to their child to help him fall asleep. I had never been read twice before by the same people.

Because they had some practice at reading me the past few days in the daytime, reading me at night was much faster. When someone read me at that speed, I would feel like I may come down with a virus or something. I have spent a few days on the shelf before my time was up. It was pretty evident that this family liked me so much. I am thankful for that.

The next day, mom and dad were getting things together for a trip to the store. Mom needed to get some more groceries and I needed to get back to the library. Dad merged the trips into one. They took me on the trip to the library while their son was in school.

This was a fun trip to their house. I learned a lot about them and their social environment. While I was at their house, I was among other books and they were of higher education level. This was a smart family.

Johnny Dean

• • •

JOHNNY WANTED TO HAVE A book to read for his upcoming trip. His family was on the move and since he was only 5 years old, he didn't know how to drive yet. He had to be chauffeured most of his young life. His family moved a few times based on the role his father played at work. Johnny was occasionally bored. They had come up with the idea of giving him a book to read for the long drives. This could only work for as long as they stayed in the same area the library was located.

Johnny's parents picked me out because they thought it was fun for him to read and maybe stay awake. They checked me out and gave me to the son. This should also keep him out of trouble. We finally arrived at his house and it looked kind of funny. Based on what I saw, there were boxes in most of the house corners. The boxes had labels on them to inform them on what goes where for their next destination.

They had me upstairs in the kid's room as I saw what was going on. There were boxes everywhere around the house. They were not in a messy situation. The messy situation was what was going in the boxes. The worst part about moving is the moving. It takes a lot of time to pack and unpack. This is why a lot of people hate doing it. This family had the uncanny position of company-moved rides.

They still had to most of the packing, but they did not have to do the loading and unloading - just the directing of it.

The move was getting a little underhanded as the day got later. Johnny was a little tired and did not want to read very much anymore that day. The parents understood this and took it under consideration. Mom had put me on top of a magazine stack. She was under the impression that if she put me in nearly plain sight, she would not lose me later.

Keeping this in mind, she tried to remember where she put me from all the ruckus that was going on.

The day had come to an end as the evening hours laid in. The movers went into the nearest motel to get some rest.

As a book, I can feel the temperature change in the air of the room. Wherever I am in the moment. By the time everything was done, I was not able to go on the road trip and had to be returned to the library. This kid never got the chance to enjoy me.

Christian Berry

• • •

THE FIVE YEAR OLD WAS going through a custody battle according to papers that I saw lying on the mother's dinner table. The mom picked me up from the library to read with her son. When we got home, the son went to his room in the single story house. The parents were in separation mode of their relationship. The next step would be coming up soon. I may be a book, but I can still read. The places of my presence added to the texture of my covers.

Christian felt an empty feeling inside because of this battle. He felt that he needed something to cover it up so it didn't show as much. That seemed to be where I came in. The problem here was that I was only there temporarily. I was only able to work there short term.

Knowing this, I may not go back because of sentimental reasons. I brought the happy thought of togetherness of the family.

This was during the night time when Christian went to bed. When they left the room, they left me on the shelf in the kid's room. A lot can often be seen from this point of view. Such things as shadows at the base of the door going across the floor were not hard to miss. The parents seemed to do their main silent fighting when Christian went to bed and fell asleep.

At least here I found out what some of the main symptoms were for the on-coming divorce. They may not have known it, but it seemed like Christian knew what was going on. This was what created the empty feeling inside. Even though the words may have been silent, the shadow fighting movement was plain and clear.

Sometimes, Christian could see it even if he was not supposed to.

One thing that the parents said they do not want to do was to hurt their child. What they did not realize was that was exactly what they were doing. The two parents each had parents that have stayed together. Where this kind of mess came from was not known. One thing was certain. This kid was not going to know what a normal family feels like unless the parents can compromise with each other.

No matter what they told Christian, it did not fill the void that he felt inside. Since the parents never went through this as a child, they did not know how he felt. What they did notice was during the night times and story times, Christian felt the happiest. The parents were side by side like the day they were married. This was what filled the void. Sometimes, something magical happened during those quiet times.

While they read me to him, they looked at each other over his head as they sat with him on his bed. The other day, as they were reading me, they were quite tired.

In the midst of reading to him, they fell asleep in his bed. He was already conked out. The husband still had some feeling in him. In the middle of the night, he had woken up and looked her way. His partner was sound asleep. He was attempting to get up without waking up anyone else.

He went over to her side of the bed and picked her up in his arms. Chivalry had not died according to this action. Under the assumption that they left the room like this, he took her to their bedroom. She was still sound asleep when they left the room. She was evidently a sound sleeper. As the night went on, it got deafly quiet. I thought this was going to be a good night.

The next morning, they had wakened and came into the kid's room to get him ready for school. Something happened last night that made a change in the course of their direction. The night held a special occasion that led to the reunion of the parents. They came in Christian's room arm in arm with each other as if the past weeks did not exist. The only reminders of such events were the boxes all over the place. Great! I bet that they would have to go through the boxes with some sort of enthusiasm. All that work just to undo it.

They decided to go with each other as they took Christian to school to go to the library and return me. This view would be boring if the scenery did not change a few times.

Samantha Broadway

ABOUT A WEEK AGO, SAMANTHA'S parents picked me up for her to read. She was showing me off in front of her friends and passing me around. They were all gathered around in a circle in her room. She was so proud of the trophy.

She was bragging about how she finished reading me in a very short time. About six or seven kids were in attendance of this sort of meeting. The kids' ages ranged from four to six. Samantha considered herself smarter than most.

She was in the middle of the group holding me in the air talking about what kind of stories that I had. The kids around her were in amazement.

Samantha liked this kind of attention. Kids of four years old are easily impressed by the older ones. One of the six-year-olds asked if they could read it next.

Samantha was not sure if that was a good idea. With that in mind, she noted that the kid's parents could pick up a copy of me at the local library.

This might have made the other kid a little envious. Probably, much to the point that there was trouble brewing in the little room.

You could see the anger in the other kids' eyes. Turf of one over the other; there was going to be a fight. The other kid got up and wanted me out of Samantha's hands.

He looked like he was going to be starting something. Reading lips, I was able to tell that Samantha was able to yell for help. The next feeling was funny.

Through Samantha's hands, I was able to feeling thumping sounds from the floor. Someone was on the way up to the room. The door came open and mom came in.

Evidently, dad was at work. This was probably a weekday. Mom came in almost storming through the door in that way where a fight needed broken up or too much noise was going on.

She wondered what was going on. When she heard of the silly nonsense, there was a sudden tug on my covers. Along with the sudden gush of wind at my cover, I think I lost some words and found someone else's.

Suddenly, I left the room in the mom's hand and wound up in her room. I wondered if she was going to start reading me since her daughter was bragging so much.

One thing that I knew for certain was that I should be safe for that moment. She put me in her foot locker with the implication or thought that the kids would not find me here.

Sometimes, when Samantha was away, like in school, she would take me out just for calmness sake. I hoped she didn't not take too long. The daughter had had me out for a week already. I was going to expire soon.

It took her a few days to finish reading me. Her daughter felt the heartfelt dismissal of a book. She missed having me and wanted me back before I went back to the library.

She came to her with puppy-dog eyes as if to mean that she was sorry for what she did. She mentioned that she was sorry when her mom was sitting at the table in the dining room.

I was on the table watching the apologetic conversation going between the two of them. She let her have me for a while just so she could be satisfied. She let her know that she had to return me soon. She understood as she had little time with me. After she was done, she sat me down in front of her mom.

The next day, mom was ready to take me back. Samantha had to go back to school again.

Timothy Masterson

THE PARENTS WENT TO THE library to pick me up. They wanted something to cheer their son up a little. They figured that I could do the trick. As soon as I got picked up by them, we had a long drive. It seemed that this was no ordinary day at the park. Our drive went all the way to the big white building. At the top of the building was a needle with a snake wrapped around it. According to some of the books at the library with a picture on the front, we were headed to a hospital.

We had to pass through a couple of double sliding doors to get to the receptionist's desk. After we signed in, we were able to get to the kid's room. Timothy was hooked up to a couple of machines. His head was bald and he was mostly under covers. It was pretty evident, by the reading of the charts that he had been diagnosed with cancer.

His parents were trying to help him out as much as they could, while they still could. Mom stayed there all night while dad had to occasionally go to work. He would get off early when he could and visit on his lunches. The dad worked as an accountant at a large firm. Sometimes his boss was not so understanding. Every time he saw his son, there was a smile on their faces. No matter how much pain they went through, the togetherness is what they cherished the most.

The doctor came in periodically to check on his patient. Evidently, there was a scheduled test to attend to. Two aides came into the room with him to help Timothy leave the room. The room they were going to was two floors up. I could see a lot from the view point of mom's hand.

I seemed to be giving her some hope that he might survive. The room was set up for chemotherapy sessions. They were not doing these sessions as an out-patient routine. The cancer was in part of the brain section. It would have been too dangerous to do the sessions out of the hospital.

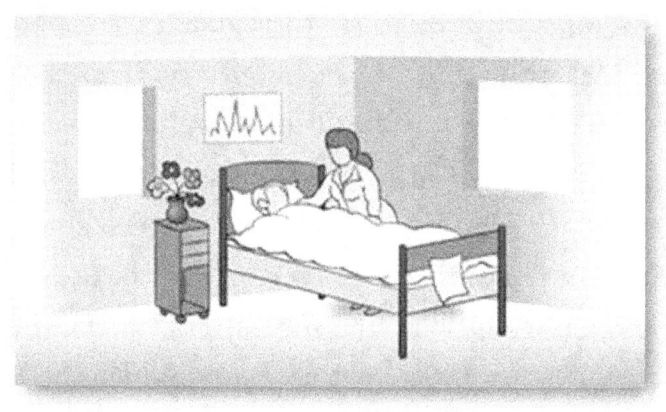

When Timothy was in the operating room, his parents were trading places back and forth reading me. This was up until the session was done. After we get back to the room, mom continued with dad in trying to make things better for him. This took a little time. During the night times, Mom would try to read him to sleep. Clearly, I was a great story book for little kids. When these nights were among us, they sometimes made mom cry. The cancer patient was the son, but it hurt the mom because it was her only son. They often spent their entire days there. For all I knew, I may have been late in getting back to the library because most of the attention was getting the son better. This I did not mind. The parents might not have minded the late fee though.

The next day, the doctor came in to find the parents taking care of their son. They were trying to get him comfortable. He let them be aware of how appreciative he was of what they were doing. This happened even though he was about to let them know that the son was going to be headed for his last chemo session. Evidently, the cancer was almost gone. They wanted to get rid of it as soon as they could.

A few hours went by since Timothy went into the room. The mom and her husband were just finishing reading me. Suddenly, the operating room doors swung open. The doctors come out and the parents waited for what could have been bad news. Mom was almost in trembling tears. She had to hold onto her husband to help keep her support in order. The doctor came up to them with the news. Obviously, Timothy made it through. Mom was smiling and holding her husband tight in joy that her son was still with her. She wanted to see him.

After he was back in the room it was possible to for them to see him. The doctor's notes were written in the angle that I could read them. The cancer node was gone and soon Timothy's hair would grow back. The hair would not be in the same style as it was before. Mom was relieved to hear the good news. She finished my stories with Timothy and proceeded to pack me up with a few other things. She was ready for a trip to run errands.

This was what happened most frequently when they were finished reading me. They took me back to the library for return. One thing was for sure.

I was able to help hold her comfort in confidence while waiting on her son to get through the cancer treatments. I shall add this to my ever-increasing history, adding a seasoning texture to my covers and pages.

Eric Jackson

• • •

THIS FIVE-YEAR-OLD WAS A CUB scout. They were on a camping trip and Eric wanted to bring me along to keep him company. There were about 30 boys going on the trip. This meant that I would be in plenty of company among other boys. The other boys had probably brought some books. One thing was, that the other kids would have more than one story book to choose from. The other books and I hoped that some respect for books and responsibility was engrained in these kids.

His parents picked me up for the ride to the scout camp. They were hoping that I could keep him entertained until the ride was over. Eric and his fellow cub scouts were camping for a week at the campground. The campground was about 30 minutes from where they lived. The camping trip was in the spring time. At least I wouldn't sweat my words off the page. The weather would be nice and cool.

I hoped that he would leave me in the campground area. One thing that I did not want to do is get damaged by the activities of the kids. Right then, I was sitting in his camping pack in the total darkness.

This was a good place for me to take a nap. It was too bad though, I already had an eight hour sleep from being in here the night before. Eric and his parents liked to prepare for events in advance.

Mom and Eric were doing their packing a week beforehand when I had been put into the bag. So far, this had been the safest place I had been in the campground.

It had been a while since the boys were gone. They should have been on their way back. Time was easy to tell sometimes when it affects my binding back. This wiggle room was pretty snug.

Eric and his friends returned and he finished unpacking the rest of his things. That included me. He set me on his pack pillow ready for a nice time at a camp fire. It was the evening time when he would bring me out. He seemed to have asked the scoutmaster about reading part of me to the boys during that time. It seemed the scoutmaster was all right with it because he nodded his head yes.

During the night, the moon was out and Eric was wearing a head attachment of a flashlight that he could read with. They were around the camp-fire with some marshmallows.

The scoutmaster was in his master chair at the head of the group. He was enjoying listening to the nighttime insects and animals in the background woods. That was what he enjoyed the most. He liked being out in the wilderness with just nature and the boys. It was a time where the boys could learn to be men.

He listened to Eric finish one of the stories with the kids. He would not dare eat a s'more with his hands on me like that. He waited until he was done reading me to have some snack desert food of his own. I appreciated that even though the heat from the fire was kind of fond of my covers.

The campfire was ending and the night wound down with a group song that all the boys seemed to have known. They were all singing in harmony and then a round of applause happened. The boys clapped themselves a goodnight.

One by one, they went to bed. The scoutmaster was in no hurry to go to bed just yet. I guess he had the responsibility of watching the fire go out before he was down for the count.

Eric had put me back in the pack for the night. I guess this meant that it was my bed time as well. That was the night that the light went out at camp. Tomorrow was another day.

I might have gotten used to this happening if I was going to be here all week.

Each time that the kids came back, they had a new merit badge to complete more of their training. Eric spent time trying to sew his new merit badges on his sash. He seemed to be doing a good job. Every time he took me out of his pack sack, I would see a new badge on him. He may become a good leader some time. The other kids with him were collecting similar and some of the same badges. When they hung their sashes up during the night time, you could watch them grow each day.

The night time had come around again. The kids were getting through with their dinners. Each of them was cooking their own meals. Some of them even had cooking merit badges. One of them was my current renter. The kids were gathering the wood to build up on the bon fire. Similar to the person writing this book, the troop normally built bon fires at the camp outs.

When the stack was high enough, the troop picked a person to light the fire from underneath. Eric had been chosen. One of the other kids was chosen for the passing of the dessert. This was an almost replica of the night before. It was almost a carbon copy. One of the only differences were that we were at a different section of me. By the time the week was over, some of the scouts were eager to re-read parts of me before it was time to go home.

Mom was very proud of her son for earning all those merit badges that he wore on his sash. He came to her and dad while they were waiting at the van. They were out of the van by the time he was about 10 feet away and closing. They gave him a hug for his accomplishments while they were there and a plan to celebrate more after they got back home.

After the camping trip was over, mom and dad got ready to return me to the library. This was a fun trip to the campgrounds. I was able to get into the outdoors without getting damaged.

The Collector

• • •

I HAVE BEEN AROUND IN several households, different cultures, different levels of living, and different environments. I could name several things to read about from where I have been. I am in a collector's possession now and ready to be preserved. Through my lifetime, I could feel the pressures of the kids that I have helped learn read. The textures of my covers represented the different handling, temperatures and places. Although I was in almost mint condition from careful handling and preservation, time has pressed into my pages like memories of lifetimes before.

Today, I sit in a similar setting of a library only these books do not get checked out. We sit for further preservations of time inducements. We are on shelves that tell stories of ages gone by and of faces that have seen the world over. If a person were to collect every type of book written, they could say that they have been everywhere. It is possible that they would be right about it.

The guy that has me on one of his shelves now is similar to that type of person. Looking around at the different book places, there is a variety of different books. Some of these books are not in English so that is a clue that they are not from around here. I know that the characters in a lot of the foreign books are different from each other. I do not have to be an expert in a different language to know of these different cultures.

If the collector has read all of these books, he has an awful lot of knowledge of different subjects. Correction: he has an awful lot of knowledge of different people's opinions of subjects. Who knows, he might have found another conclusion or theory of his own by reading what other people had to say.

He had been in the collection business for a long time. Some of these books are dating way back in the 19th century. He is a collector for sure. It's like he goes out searching for unique and out-of-the-ordinary books. These books do not look similar to ones that I have seen before. Some of the unique characteristics are separating themselves from others.

Sometimes, the owner comes in to see his collection or to add others. It is easy to see that he is definitely not done. He has dozens and dozens of shelves, but only a few of them have books filled to the tip. The books were organized in the way of his own system. If he organized them in any ordinary way, he would have to keep adjusting all the rest of the books from a certain point. That was the reason for his own system. But, if I stay in this collection long enough then I might find out what that system is.

When I came in, I saw clip boards of paper on some of the individual book cases.

Evidently, each case is its own system. Still, I do not know what they are. My shelf is almost complete. The room is temperature controlled which is a good thing. The owner just has to come in and put the new-to-him books into his system, set them on one of the shelves, and walk out.

A couple of windows shine in on us. They are not clear windows but they are nice to the sun. They provide those black crisscross lines to show what kind of windows they are. Only a few of them are actually for this room. I guess you do not need a magnifying glass to shine in on these books textures. A magnifying glass, such as a clear window, will actually start a fire if directed at paper. We cannot have that. From this perspective, I can say that we, the other books and I, are protectively in preservation.

Thank you for reading my stories and have a nice nap.

The End.